SHARK DOG!

Ged Adamson

HARPER
An Imprint of HarperCollins Publishers

ISBN 978-0-06-2457134 (trade bdg.)
The artist used pencil and watercolor paints to create the illustrations for this book.
Typography by Jeanne L. Hogle
17 18 19 20 21 SCP 10 9 8 7 6 5 4 3 2 1

First Edition

For Rex

My dad is no ordinary dad. He's a famous explorer who travels the world. Sometimes, I get to tag along.

On one trip, when we were busy exploring, we found beautiful butterflies and strange plants, tortoises as big as cars, and colorful birds in huge trees.

And yet . . . on that trip I had a strange feeling I was being followed.

As we sailed home, I thought I heard a loud noise.

Later that night, something woke me from a deep,
peaceful sleep. Something slobbery!

I turned on the light and saw the strangest creature—
half dog and half shark.

He seemed friendly enough, so
Dad said I could keep him.

Back on land, Shark Dog made himself right at home.
And he began to do his *own* exploring.

It didn't exactly go as planned.

And at the park, we didn't stay long.

Shark Dog was no ordinary pet.

Sometimes, when he did dog things,
he was more like a shark.

And sometimes, when he did shark things, he was more like a dog.

SCRUNCH!

Either way, Shark Dog was a fun friend to have around. On land.

And underwater.

We did everything together.

"Sweet dreams, Shark Dog."

What Shark Dog loved most was a trip to the beach.

It was important to keep an eye on him
at all times, because . . .

. . . when people spot a fin sticking out of the water,
they do get a little bit worried.

Being near water always made Shark Dog super excited.

One time, Shark Dog was more excited
than I'd ever seen him.

He'd spotted another shark dog!

He couldn't contain his joy.

But it wasn't another shark dog. And for the first time,
my Shark Dog was sad.

He was still sad that evening.

He was even sadder the next day.

And the day after that.

"Oh no!" I said to my dad. "I bet Shark Dog is thinking about his home."

"Maybe it's time we took him back," said Dad.

So we did.

Shark Dog got the most wonderful welcome.

My dad even took his friends out for a ride.
It was a happy day.

That night, the shark dogs sang us a
beautiful song in the moonlight.

The next morning, it was hard to say good-bye,
but I told Shark Dog it was time to go.

Suddenly Shark Dog began to follow our boat.

Then, with one enormous leap, he was back on board!

"I think Shark Dog made his mind up," said Dad.

"It looks like you're his home now."
And that was just fine with me.

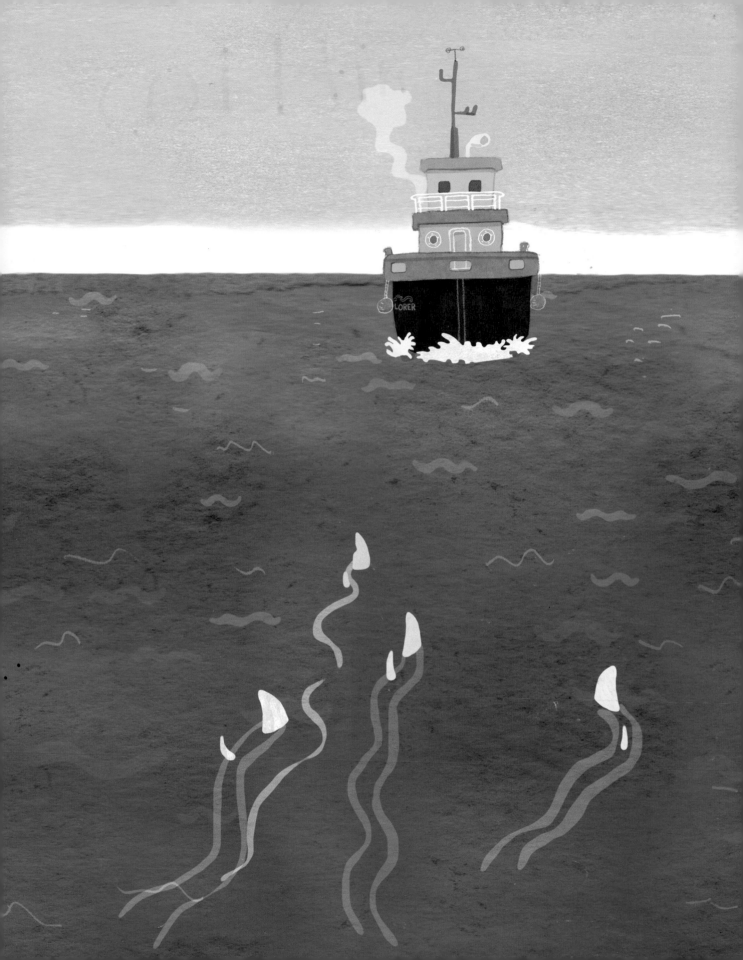